WOODRIDGE PUBLIC LIBRARY
W9-BYB-260
3 1524 00[illegible]4

J
Kudlinski

Kudlinski, Kathleen V.

Facing west.

DATE

APR 13 1995
APR 24 1995
JUN 09 1995
JUL 24 1995
AUG 14 1995
SEP 06 1995
OCT 04 1995
FEB 15 1996
MAR 11 1996
MAR 31 1997
SEP 26 1997
JUL 02 1998
JUL 27 1998

WOODRIDGE PUBLIC LIBRARY
3 PLAZA DRIVE
WOODRIDGE, IL 60517-2099
(708) 964-7899

WITHDRAWN
Woodridge Public Library

BAKER & TAYLOR

OCT 1994

The ONCE UPON AMERICA® Series

A LONG WAY TO GO
A Story of Women's Right to Vote

HERO OVER HERE
A Story of World War I

IT'S ONLY GOODBYE
An Immigrant Story

THE DAY IT RAINED FOREVER
A Story of the Johnstown Flood

PEARL HARBOR IS BURNING!
A Story of World War II

HANNAH'S FANCY NOTIONS
A Story of Industrial New England

CHILD STAR
When Talkies Came to Hollywood

THE BITE OF THE GOLD BUG
A Story of the Alaskan Gold Rush

FIRE!
The Beginnings of the Labor Movement

NIGHT BIRD
A Story of the Seminole Indians

CLOSE TO HOME
A Story of the Polio Epidemic

HARD TIMES
A Story of the Great Depression

EARTHQUAKE!
A Story of Old San Francisco

THE PRESIDENT IS DEAD
A Story of the Kennedy Assassination

TOUGH CHOICES
A Story of the Vietnam War

RED MEANS GOOD FORTUNE
A Story of San Francisco's Chinatown

LONE STAR
A Story of the Texas Rangers

FACING WEST
A Story of the Oregon Trail

BEAUTIFUL LAND
A Story of the Oklahoma Land Rush

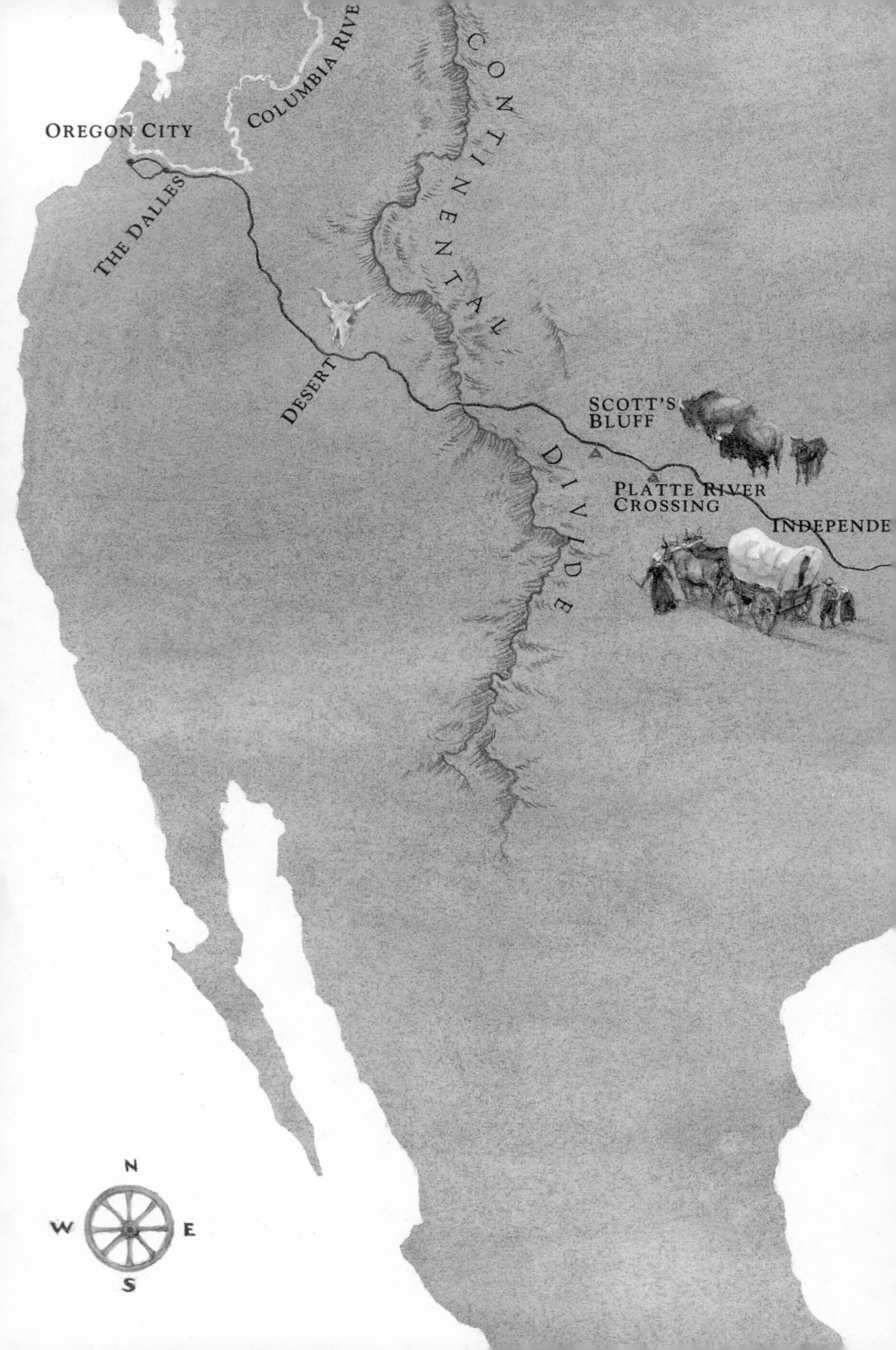
COLUMBIA RIVE
OREGON CITY
THE DALLES
CONTINENTAL
DIVIDE
DESERT
SCOTT'S BLUFF
PLATTE RIVER CROSSING
INDEPENDE
N
W
E
S

Facing West

A STORY OF THE OREGON TRAIL

BY KATHLEEN V. KUDLINSKI

ILLUSTRATED BY JAMES WATLING

VIKING

WOODRIDGE PUBLIC LIBRARY

To my parents, Grace and William Veenis

Many thanks to Sarah Le Compte, historian at the National Historic Oregon Trail Center, and Linda Waldeman, M.D., pediatric specialist, who read this text for background authenticity. And a special thanks to Barbara Kenney and James Watling.

VIKING
Published by the Penguin Group
Penguin Books USA Inc., 375 Hudson Street, New York, New York 10014, U.S.A.
Penguin Books Ltd, 27 Wrights Lane, London W8 5TZ, England
Penguin Books Australia Ltd, Ringwood, Victoria, Australia
Penguin Books Canada Ltd, 10 Alcorn Avenue, Toronto, Ontario, Canada M4V 3B2
Penguin Books (N.Z.) Ltd, 182–190 Wairau Road, Auckland 10, New Zealand

Penguin Books Ltd, Registered Offices: Harmondsworth, Middlesex, England

First published in 1994 by Viking, a division of Penguin Books USA Inc.

1 3 5 7 9 10 8 6 4 2

Text copyright © Kathleen V. Kudlinski, 1994
Illustrations copyright © James Watling, 1994
All rights reserved

Library of Congress Cataloging-in-Publication Data
Kudlinski, Kathleen V.
Facing west : a story of the Oregon Trail / by Kathleen V. Kudlinski : illustrated by James Watling.
p. cm. —(Once upon America)
Summary: As his family sets out from Missouri to Oregon, young Ben wonders whether he will have more trouble with the dangers of the journey or his debilitating asthma.
ISBN 0-670-85451-4
1. Oregon Trail—Juvenile fiction. [1. Oregon Trail—Fiction. 2. Overland journeys to the Pacific—Fiction. 3. Frontier and pioneer life—West (U.S.)—Fiction. 4. Asthma—Fiction.] I. Watling, James, ill. II. Title. III. Series.
PZ7.K9486Fac 1994 [Fic]—dc20 93-41349 CIP AC

ONCE UPON AMERICA® is a registered trademark of Viking Penguin, a division of Penguin Books USA Inc.
Printed in U.S.A. Set in 12 pt. Goudy Old Style
Without limiting the rights under copyright reserved above, no part of this publication may be reproduced, stored in or introduced into a retrieval system, or transmitted, in any form or by any means (electronic, mechanical, photocopying, recording or otherwise), without the prior written permission of both the copyright owner and the above publisher of this book.

Contents

The Elephant

"Are you ready to look for the elephant, Bear Cub?"

Ben's head spun around and he stared at the stranger. He could feel his mouth fall open. The man was all fur and fringe, topped with a coonskin cap. Wild black hair hung below his shoulders, and a beard covered his chest. Leather strings swung from his beaded shirt. The man was big, and he smelled bad, too. Ben thought he must have missed his Saturday baths for a year. Maybe longer.

"My name's Pete," the stranger said. "I'll be leading your wagon train across to Oregon Territory."

Ben jumped to his feet. "You know the way? You've been there? Is it as wonderful as they say?" His questions spilled out. "Is the air clear? Is the trail really so dangerous?"

"Whoa, there, Bear Cub." Pete held up his hands. "One question at a time is all an old mountain man like me can get a handle on."

Ben thought for a moment. "How dangerous is the trail?" he asked. That was the worry that had kept him up all night. "Are we going to make it?"

"Well, now, that's hard to say." The mountain man pulled on his mustache. "If you don't die of hunger or thirst, if your wagon doesn't roll off a cliff or wash down a river, if you don't die of camp sickness, if you don't get eaten by wild Indians, if the rattlesnakes and bears don't crawl into your bed some night, well, then you'll make it. Maybe."

Ben shivered. That's what he was afraid of. His family was going to Oregon. They were going to die on the way, and it was all his fault. His chest felt tight. It was a feeling he hated.

"Everybody faces something along the trail," Pete went on, "something awful. They call it 'seeing the elephant.' Most folks face it down and live to tell the tale. Others die trying."

Ben was sorry he had asked.

Pete looked off to the east, raised his pistol and fired it into the sky. Ben jumped. Then he heard pistols being fired all along the wagon train.

"Sun's up, Bear Cub. Time to get the wagons all ready to roll," Pete said. "Keep an eye out for elephants, now." And he headed off through the early spring grass toward the horses.

"Ben!" Mama's voice called through the canvas roof of their new wagon. "How could you wander off like that? What if you'd had a bad breathing spell out on the prairie?"

"Sorry, Mama," Ben said quietly. The doctor had told them he could have a spell anywhere, anytime now. He almost wished he could just stop breathing. That way he wouldn't have to worry about it anymore.

"Your big sister is getting firewood. You sit down and mind the kettle while I dress Becky. Here—" his mother held out a book. "Write in the journal. It will be your daily chore for the trip. Nobody else will have time."

Ben didn't want to write, today or any other day. He didn't like writing. He wanted to explore the wagon train. Their boat had pulled into Independence, Missouri, only yesterday. Pa had met a family on the dock that wanted to quit and go home before they even began the trip west. "Go-backs" Pa called them.

He bought their wagon and gear. Suddenly Ben and his family were on their way to Oregon.

"The sooner we get started," Pa had said, "the better we'll have it along the way. After all these other wagon trains hit the trail, there won't be any firewood left for us or grass for our cows to graze."

So the Clarks had moved their new wagon, their new oxen and cows, their new chickens and geese into place and left for Oregon. Pa always made up his mind that fast.

Ben sat by the cook fire and opened the journal to the first page. Amanda walked up and dropped a pile of firewood with a crash. She glared at him and stamped away. "It isn't my fault" he wanted to yell after his sister. "I didn't ask to have asthma!" He fought his tears. Eleven-year-olds didn't cry. Besides, it could start a bad spell.

April 18, 1845, he wrote, and stopped. What else should he write? Who would ever read it? He would probably not survive the trip, anyhow. The asthma would get him. He'd end up under one of those little crosses he'd heard about on the trail. They'd bury the book with him, he supposed. And his jackknife. A teardrop hit the blank page.

"Howdy, partner!" a boy's voice called across the campfire. Ben quickly wiped his eyes. "Smoke makes my eyes water up, too," the boy said and grinned. "My name's Zack."

"I'm Ben." He smiled at Zack. He couldn't help it. He'd never seen so many freckles on one face before. Or, he thought, such pale yellow hair.

"I'm glad your family is along instead of the folks who owned this wagon before," Zack said. "They only had five girls—nobody to have adventures with."

"You have adventures?" Ben asked.

"Every day," Zack said. "If I don't find them, I make them."

"Ben, are you finished writing yet?" Mama climbed out of the wagon and helped Becky get down.

"Almost, Mama," Ben lied. "This is Zack."

"Zachariah Mulberry, at your service, ma'am," Zack said, bowing low. His eyes twinkled as they caught Ben's. "My mother sends her best wishes and asks you to drop by at any time."

"What a nice boy that is," Mama said after Zack left.

Ben sat and watched as she made breakfast. Then he took out his knife and sharpened his pencil. *Day one. We begin the ride to Oregon*, he wrote. There was too much crowding his mind to write—and all of it was bad. Their hurried start. That strange man, Pete. Elephant-sized dangers. Asthma. Little crosses. You can't start a journal that way, he scolded himself, even if it is all true. Finally he remembered Zack and wrote, *I might have found a friend today.*

Pa walked up and took a plateful of eggs and bacon.

He grinned at his wife. "The cows ate well, the oxen are fresh, the sun is shining, and our family is together. We're off to take Oregon!"

"And you'll get your farm at last." Mama reached across the breakfast cloth and held his hand.

Ben looked away. They had left the house and carpenter shop Pa had built in Saint Louis because of him, and he knew it. The doctor had said the air out west was healthier.

"I'll go get water," he said.

"No, son." Mama shook her head. "Your sister will do it while you feed the chickens." Amanda grabbed the bucket, glared, and stamped off. "You take the last piece of bacon." Mama handed it to Ben.

When the dishes were done and the oxen hitched up, Mrs. Clark drove the wagon into line. "Is this our place for the whole trip?" Amanda said. "I like being in the middle of 60 wagons!"

"No," Mr. Clark said. He was riding beside them on Gray, the farm horse they'd bought from the go-backs. "We move up one place every day until we hit the front. Then we go to the back and work up again."

"That's better," Ben said. "Everyone has a turn at the tail and at the head of the train. I'm going to like this."

But he didn't. "Sit up there Ben," Mama said. Amanda and Becky were already in the wagon. Papa had ridden to the back of the wagon train to herd their

new cattle. Ben was just sitting down as the oxen started to pull. The whole wagon jerked forward, and knocked his head against the blanket chest. The wagon rolled and bounced, jolted and bumped over the trail.

He tried holding himself stiff. He tried sitting limp. He tried leaning. Standing. Lying back against the wooden bench. Nothing helped.

"You haven't been getting much exercise, that's why it hurts so," Mama said.

That's not my fault. Ben was hurting so much that he almost said it aloud. He remembered all the times Mama had made him walk when he wanted to run. Wait when he wanted to hurry. Sit when he wanted to explore. All because of his breathing. He wiggled again.

"Get out!" Mama finally said. "Try walking."

Two hours later, the train halted for the noon break. The oxen needed an hour's rest. So did Ben. He sat down on a box to eat his cold biscuits, then stood up quickly. I was wrong, he thought. Day one. We begin the *walk* to Oregon.

Adventure

May 10, 1845, Ben wrote. He stared into the breakfast fire, then added, *The same as yesterday and the day before and the day before that*. One whole month on the Oregon trail and nothing had changed. The sky, the land, the chores, the people, and the endless walking were always the same. Even if he liked writing, there wouldn't be any more to write about. He threw his pencil down and climbed a wagon wheel to look back over the prairie.

"What do you see?" Zack climbed up beside him and leaned against the dusty gray canvas.

"Aren't those the fire circles where we camped yesterday?" Ben pointed far back over the cattle grazing in the hot morning sun. Zack nodded. "How can you walk eighteen long miles," Ben complained, "and not seem to get anywhere?"

"Isn't it grand!" Zack said. Ben was silent. He hadn't thought of it that way. "Look, just *look* at all the wagons!" Chains of white wagon covers strung across the prairie behind them, shining in the sun.

"I like being the very last wagon of our train," Ben said. "It seems like I'm closer to home." He thought about the big oak outside his bedroom window. About how he used to climb it to sneak in and out of the house. Before the asthma. Before the trip.

"You're wrong," Zack said. "In two months, you'll be at the front of the train again. *Then* you'll be closer to home—your new home."

Ben jumped down. "Let's *do* something," he said.

Zack grinned. He put his finger to his lips and crawled under the wagon. He lay down in the tall grass and crawled toward the rise.

"Where are we going?" Ben whispered. Zack just shook his head and kept crawling. Ben followed, ready for adventure.

At the top of the ridge, Zack whispered, "The women," and pointed ahead.

Ben's mouth fell open. There were no outhouses on the plains. No trees. Not even bushes to hide behind if you needed privacy. When you had a need, you stepped behind a wagon—and hoped nobody was watching. It was awful.

Amanda, Becky, Mama, and the other women wandered off together every morning to take care of their needs. Men weren't supposed to follow. Boys either. Especially boys. Ben couldn't imagine what would happen to them if they were caught.

On wash days, he'd seen how ladies' pantaloons were open between their legs. He felt his cheeks burn red when he thought about it. He decided that he wouldn't even peek, and he didn't—until Zack said, "So that's how they do it."

Ben couldn't help himself. He swallowed hard and poked his head over the rise. Below him, the women had made a circle, all facing out. They spread their skirts wide and made a wall. There was Mama, the minister's wife, the blacksmith's daughters, and Zack's grandmother. One by one, each woman turned and squatted down inside, hidden by the wall of skirts. Then each came out and took her place in the circle again. Ben watched in breathless silence.

"Howdy, Bear Cubs," a deep voice said behind them. Ben's heart stopped. His eyes met Zack's as he slowly turned. They were in terrible trouble. Ben felt it in his bones. Zack showed it on his face.

"Trying out your scouting skills, boys?" It was Pete, standing quietly beside his horse. His face looked serious. Then suddenly he was smiling. Ben let his breath out. The boys wiggled back down the rise and stood up. They grinned, then giggled. They laughed until Ben felt his chest get tight.

Finally, Pete coughed and they were quiet again. "Ben," Pete asked, "are you having trouble here at the back of the train?"

"No, sir," Ben answered. *Trouble? Here?*

Pete nodded, then looked at the sun. "You might today. It's going to be a hot one. I'll be back to see you later." Pete mounted his horse and rode off.

"Are you a friend of his?" Zack's surprise showed in his voice.

"No. He talks to my mama sometimes, but I don't think he likes people much."

"Seems that way. He always rides away before noon. He never sits by anybody's campfire in the night. Nobody knows where he goes."

"He said some strange things to me the first day of the trip." Ben remembered the nightmares he'd had about bears and snakes and elephants in his bed.

"He smells bad, too," Zack said. "But he sure can ride."

They watched Pete gallop out along the trail. His pinto was a small horse, but strong. He had to be strong, Ben thought, the way Pete rode him.

"Wouldn't you love to push on ahead of everybody like that?" he asked Zack.

"Let's roll!" the train's captain, Mr. Tyler, called. Zack ran to his own wagon. The women came back from their morning walk through the grasses. Ben looked at the ground. He felt the blood rush to his cheeks.

He hurried to put out the morning fire. Then he called, "Becky!" Those were his chores: the fire and his little sister. It was stupid work for a boy, but it was all Mama would let him do. He threw the leftover twigs and dry cow droppings into the blanket hanging under the wagon. They'd burn them in the noon fire. Pa argued the oxen back into their places, and the family faced west. The big wheels turned with a screech and the harnesses jingled. The children began the day's march.

"I'm tired," Becky said as they started.

"Come on now." Ben took her hand. "Today's walk will be easy."

But it wasn't. Before an hour had passed, the sun dried the soil to dust. The ironclad wheels of 59 wagons crushed the dry grasses to a powder. Clouds of dust hung in the air by the time the Clarks' wagon finally passed.

"Carry me," Becky begged.

Ben didn't answer. He couldn't. The dust made his throat hurt. His chest felt tight and sore. And a tickle

was teasing, deep inside. Don't start coughing, Ben told himself. Just don't start. The dust filled his nose and coated his tongue.

Ben began breathing in short little breaths. He wanted to fill his lungs, but he couldn't pull the air in. He couldn't move the old air out, either. The short little breaths got faster, and they made a whistling sound. He needed more air.

"Carry me, Ben," Becky pleaded.

"No." Ben spoke quickly. "Not. Now." He tried not to cough, but it was starting. He could feel it coming. He coughed once to stop the tickle and then he couldn't stop.

"Get me some water," Becky said. "I'm hot."

Ben fought to breathe. The harder he coughed, the less air he got, and the more scared he was. His face felt cold, and he was getting dizzy. Air. He needed air.

"Mama!" he heard Becky yell. "Ben's face is all white!"

Pa ran to help Ben up into the wagon. Ben sat beside Mama on the wooden seat, coughing and coughing. "Just relax," Mama said.

Relax? Ben fought for air. He couldn't breathe!

"Give the Bear Cub to me." He heard Pete's voice from a distance. "I'll ride out of the dust with him. That will help."

Ben felt Pa's hands under his arms. He was being

lifted. Then he was on Pete's horse. Ben was coughing, coughing. Under him, the horse was galloping.

He closed his eyes and leaned back against Pete's chest. He started breathing in time to the horse's hooves. Then it was easier. And then he could breathe more deeply. When he opened his eyes, the wagons—and the dust—were gone. The horse was rushing across the prairie, and clean, sweet air was coming into Ben's lungs.

He tried to take a deep breath and started coughing again. "Whoa," Pete said. His horse slowed. "Try this, Ben." Pete coughed twice in a row. Ben felt the coughs with his whole body. They were deep and sharp. Pete waited a minute. Then he coughed twice again. Waited. Did it again.

"The first cough loosens it all up," he said as the pinto walked along. "The second one gets it out. You can spit or swallow, doesn't matter to me."

Ben tried it. "How did you know to do that?" he asked, when he could get his breath.

"I had asthma, too, when I was a cub. It's pretty near gone now, but I still can't stand the dust of a wagon train."

Ben remembered seeing him ride away every day. "And it's not just dust, is it? It's smoke, too. That's why you stay away from campfires, isn't it?"

"Smoke used to trigger the asthma for me. Buffalo-chip smoke, especially. Happens now about as often as it snows in July."

"I thought it only got worse. I thought it would just happen to me over and over and over, forever." Ben could feel the sting of tears behind his eyes—and the sick tightness growing again in his chest.

"Maybe it will and maybe it won't. Don't borrow tomorrow's troubles, Cub. It only muddies up today."

Muddy, Ben thought. He liked that picture. That was exactly what his days had been like. Muddy. Having asthma was like having to walk in deep mud all the time.

"You just stay upwind of campfires, you hear?" Pete said. "And I'll come get you on dusty days." He pulled his horse to a stop along a rise. "Now look yonder." A river wandered wide and flat and brown below them. "That's the Platte."

Ben whistled. "We really *are* getting somewhere!"

Indian Attack

"Don't hit my arm again!" Ben shook his pencil at Amanda. "You made me write *June 6, 1841*, instead of *1845*!"

He wanted to get everything down right, so he'd remember just the way it was. After two months, this was the first time they'd taken a day off. No endlessly creaking wheels. No snapping whips. No walking! Ben leaned back against a wagon wheel and propped the journal against his knees. *We are in a river of buffalo*, he wrote. *They are walking past, around the wagons. There must be a thousand of them*. He crossed out *thousand* and wrote *million*.

The huge animals were just passing by, stopping to graze, then moving on. They didn't seem to feel the harsh wind that had swept over the train for weeks now. They didn't seem to see the train, either.

They are so noisy! Their hooves thud and their bellies rumble. They grind their teeth, too. I can hear buffalo belches and breaths and snores. And they bellow and moo at each other all the time.

Ben knew it wasn't good writing. He didn't care. He wanted to save this and someday tell somebody what it was like. Maybe he'd copy it over and send it back to his uncle in Chicago. Maybe he'd mail it to a newspaper.

And they stink! Dirty wool, fresh wet buffalo chips and puddles, stomach gas. The ground is the only good smell. After all their hooves dig it up, it smells like a new-plowed field.

Ben faced west. The herd of buffalo was still coming, walking in clumps and alone, cows and little calves, bulls and yearlings.

Their hair is so long in front that you can't see their eyes or horns. And their back halves look like Pa shaved each and every one of them! Buffalo calves are as big as cows. The bulls look as big as elephants.

Ben stopped trying to show the buffalos in words. Instead he drew a sketch in his journal. "Not bad!" he said out loud, then looked around quickly. Amanda didn't stop sewing. Mama was still down at the river with Becky, washing clothes. He started writing again.

Pa and the other men went out to hunt first thing this morning. Pete had told them that buffalo were near.

"Have you seen the guards?" Amanda stopped sewing. "There should be more than two men here." She threw the shirt she'd been working on into the back of the wagon. She yanked another out of the mending bag. "What if they come for us while all the other men are gone?"

Ben didn't have to ask who "they" were. They were the Indians. Amanda was terrified of them. Everybody had been, at the start. People had told horrible stories around the campfires, posted extra lookouts, and kept every gun loaded and ready. Two months had gone by with no sign of Indians, so their fears had faded. All except Amanda's.

"The cowhands could help in an attack," Ben said.

"They're too busy keeping the cows from joining the buffalo, Ben. Or they've gone over the hill to shoot a few for themselves." She was right, he thought. When Pete said that shooting near the wagons might start a stampede, almost all the men had grabbed their guns and ridden far off into the herd.

Amanda sighed and looked at the hills again.

"Well," Ben said, "At least I'm here."

"You?" Amanda said. "What are *you* good for? As

soon as you start to do a lick of work, your breathing gets funny. Or Mama tells you to stop—and then she tells me to do it instead."

Ben stared at her. He and Amanda often fought, but this was different.

"You're worse than useless," she went on. "You're spoiled. Mama gives you all the coffee you want when you're having a spell. You get teas and treats that nobody else gets." Her voice was shaking. "You don't have to gather buffalo chips all day long. And you don't even have to walk in the dust like the rest of us."

Amanda reached into the sewing bag. Ben ducked and covered his head with the journal. His sister's aim was good when she got mad.

"It's not fair! It's not fair." She choked. Ben looked over the book. Amanda was sobbing, her face stuffed into a ripped petticoat.

Ben didn't know what to say. He reached out to her. "Go away." She pulled away. "Just go away."

Ben walked silently out toward the buffalo. Is she right? he asked himself. He stared out at Scottsbluff. It had been so exciting to see the big landmarks at first. Chimney Rock. Then Courthouse Rock. He'd sketched each one in his journal.

Now the towering landmarks just looked cold and distant. Ben took out his knife and picked up a broken spoke from a wagon wheel. The oak was so dry and hard that the blade could barely cut it.

He threw the spoke away as hard as he could. "It's not my fault," he whispered to the endless, dry wind. "I don't want asthma. I don't want to be spoiled. I don't want any of it." He picked up an old dry piece of buffalo droppings and threw it, too.

"I'm *not* useless," Ben said aloud. He just wished he knew what he was good *for*. He threw another buffalo chip, harder. He ought to be gathering them for tonight's fire, he thought. Any other boy would. He threw another.

"A fine shot!" Ben turned to see Zack. His friend reached down for a chip, and Ben grabbed one, too. Instead of throwing it off toward the bluff, he hit Zack with it.

"What?" Zack stood up in surprise, and Ben slammed him with another one. Zack looked angry for a minute, then grinned. "If it's war you want . . ."

Zack's throw hit Ben's head, and the battle was on. The boys stooped to grab chips as they ran, stopping only to fire them at each other. The oldest, driest chips burst into flakes as they hit. Their dust swept away like smoke on the wind. Fresher chips hit harder. The battle was silent at first.

Then it got loud. "Gotcha!" Zack would yell, or "Good shot!" Then the laughter started.

Ben shot one at Zack's knees, then crouched low. Zack ran on. He turned, raised his arm to throw, and froze. "Oh, no!" he cried.

A buffalo chip flew past Ben's head and plopped into Zack's gut. "Ooof!" Zack scooped another chip.

Ben turned to see their attackers. An Indian? An Indian boy and Pete! A damp chip smacked into his cheek. He ducked to grab another chip. It didn't make sense, but there was no time to figure it out now. Pete and the boy were throwing chips at them—and their aim was deadly.

One hit Ben's shoulder and nearly spun him around. "No fair!" he yelled. "Pete, you're too strong!" His answer was a soggy *plop* on the other shoulder. Ben pulled up a dry chip and knocked Pete's hat off.

Pete just laughed and kept fighting.

The battle lasted until all four stood panting in the sunshine. Pete raised his hand. " 'Nuff, Bear Cubs," he said. Then he said something to the native boy in a language Ben had never heard.

Ben thought the boy was about his age. "How!" he said, and held up his hand. The boy just laughed and said something to Pete. The mountain man nodded.

"He says with what you've got on your hands, you'd better not greet too many people that way," Pete explained.

Ben looked down at his hands and hooted. "Maybe we'd better wash up," he said. He could just imagine what his mother would say. And what would Amanda think about the Indian? He looked more closely at the boy. The boy was looking him over, too.

"Saka just wanted to see a white boy close up," Pete explained. "I told him I had several I was keeping prisoner. Me powerful warrior, see?"

Zack knocked his hat off with another chip.

Ben watched the Indian walk into the muddy water of the Platte River. "Wait for me!" he yelled. He pulled off his boots and socks, slipped his suspenders down, dropped his pants, unbuttoned his cuffs, and pulled his shirt over his head.

"You should dress like the Sioux!" Pete called. Ben wished he could. The Indian was wearing a wide strip of soft leather pulled up between his legs. It was tied with a string around his waist. That was it, plus moccasins just like Pete's.

Ben pushed up the sleeves of his long johns and waded into the river. Saka kicked water into his face. The battle went on until Pete had to take the boy back to the Sioux hunting camp. "It's just beyond the bluff," he explained as they climbed onto their horses. "I lived with this tribe for years, back before you were a wiggler." He looked at Ben's face. "Don't worry, Bear Cub. I'll be back in time to set off with the wagons tomorrow."

The boys let the hot wind dry out their long johns while they walked back to the train. "First time I've felt cool in a month!" Ben said when they stopped to dress.

Zack looked up at the sun and shook his head. "I'd better get some chips for the supper fire."

Ben didn't have to do that. It was Amanda's chore. Like most everything else, he thought.

He stood for a moment looking at Scottsbluff. Then he reached down and started gathering chips.

The Divide

"Jake's down!" Mama screamed. The wagon jerked as the ox dropped to his knees. Becky fell off the tailgate. Tinware crashed to the floor inside the wagon. A bucket fell and rolled back down the mountainside.

"Dang!" Pa swore. He threw his whip to the ground and ran to the fallen ox.

"I'll get the rocks, Pa!" Ben yelled. He didn't have to look far. He jammed one behind each wheel, trying not to hear Becky's cries.

"What happened?" Amanda called weakly.

"Jake tripped, honey, that's all." Mama said. Her voice was full of worry. "Now, don't you get up."

Ben ran to Becky. "It hurts, Benny," she cried, "Oh, it hurts!" She hugged her arm tight.

Mama pressed her hand to her head. "Ben, can you take care of Becky? Jake needs water."

"Yes, Mama." Ben watched as she walked back uphill. Her dress hung loose as an empty flour sack. When did she get so skinny? Ben hugged Becky and rocked her carefully.

"What's happening?" Amanda cried from her cot in the wagon.

"Nothing to worry about," Ben answered.

She had gotten skinny, too, he thought. But that was because of the cholera. Amanda had been weak ever since she took sick last month. At least it hadn't killed her. Mrs. Simmons had died of the disease. So had Mr. March, and every one of the Cuthbert children. Ben remembered the little row of crosses they'd left behind that day. He shivered and hugged Becky tighter.

"Oooow!" she wailed.

The next team pulled up behind Ben. Mrs. Cuthbert hurried over. For a change, she wasn't crying. "Let me see it, Becky," she said. She ran her hands over the little girl's arm. It was black and blue already, and swollen. She looked at Ben. "Get your mother," she said. "I think it's broken."

Ben walked uphill to the head of the team. Jake lay as he had fallen. The big white ox's front legs were folded beneath him and his head was lying on the ground. There was pain in his dark eyes. Mama tried to pour a dipper of water into his mouth. The heavy ox yoke was nearly pulling Sam, Jake's brown teammate, over.

"I'll do that," Ben said. "Becky needs you." Mama looked into his eyes for a moment and handed him the dipper.

Pa struggled to get Sam out of the twisted harness so the brown ox could hold his neck straight again. Sam shook his head and bellowed. "Drat!" Pa swore, as his fingers were squeezed between the yoke and the ox's neck. "You stupid cuss!"

"Heave away!" Mr. Cuthbert shouted. Together the two men freed the oxen. Soon a crowd gathered around Jake.

"Try and walk him. That'll get the kinks out," one man said.

"Shoot him. He always was a sorry ox," someone else said. "I knew he'd fall, first time I see'd him."

"We'll just leave you folks here. Catch up when you can."

"No!" Pete's voice called out. "Wagon trains stay together!"

"We'll hold noon break right here," the captain of the train said. "Then we'll decide what to do."

Pa stood talking with the captain. The other men left. Mama put Becky's arm in a sling. Then she pulled out jerky and cold biscuits left from breakfast for the noon meal.

Ben rubbed the worn spots on Sam's neck and led him off the trail. He didn't need the whip to move the ox toward fresh grass. All the animals were hungry. Ben chewed a piece of dried buffalo meat as he pulled up tough mountain plants for Jake. When he carried them back to the wagon, his chest began to hurt.

Not now! he thought. He didn't need an asthma spell now—not with Amanda sick and Becky hurt. Ben felt the worry growing and fought it back. He sat down and leaned against Jake's side.

Ben let his head and shoulders droop. He breathed in slowly through his nose the way Pete had told him to. When he breathed out, he held his lips like he was going to whistle. He blew silently and slowly instead.

Instead of thinking about breathing, he looked at the land. The South Pass where they were traveling was wide and grassy, but huge mountains and cliffs went on and on to the north. Even though it was the Fourth of July, some of the mountains were covered with snow. To the south were more mountains. Back toward Saint Louis were low hills and plains. Ahead, the trail kept climbing. We must be near the top by now, Ben thought.

This land, this sky, these mountains are so big that they

make you feel like a flea. . . . He worked out the words he'd use later in his journal. A *flea on an elephant. The flea knows he's alive, but the elephant doesn't care.* Thinking ahead about the writing made it easier. His pictures were getting better and better, too. Even Pete said so. Ben took a deep, easy breath. It had worked! He smiled and got up to fetch more food for the oxen.

"No! I've had enough!" Angry words were coming from the Cuthberts' wagon. Ben tried not to listen.

"But we're almost halfway." That was Mr. Cuthbert. Only halfway? Ben was surprised.

"But my babies, my poor babies," Mrs. Cuthbert cried. "And now I'm going to have a new one," she went on. "I won't give another child of mine to the trail. I won't."

There was quiet, then Mrs. Cuthbert said, "If we turn back now, we could be home before it is born." The way she said *home* made Ben long for his old room and his St. Louis friends.

"Benjamin!" Pa yelled. "Come to the wagon!"

All of the Clarks were there, gathered around Jake. The ox was down again. His chin lay on the grass Ben had pulled up for him. This time Jake's eyes did not hold pain.

They held death.

Mama looked as if she might cry.

"What happened?" Ben asked. He rubbed his hand

over the ox's side. He could count the ribs right through the skin. "He was sick, wasn't he?" Jake's hooves were nearly worn down, too.

"I should have known. For weeks Jake hasn't been pulling his own share of the weight," Pa said. "And this South Pass climbs so slow and easy it didn't seem hard—except to the oxen."

"We're done then, aren't we?" Mama said. "Sam can't pull the wagon alone." She sighed and faced west. "It's over, isn't it?"

"I'm afraid so," Pa said it so low that Ben almost didn't hear it. "I should have bought another team when we stopped at Fort Laramie. I just don't know enough about animals."

Mama sighed again. Becky leaned into her skirt and started to cry. "I don't want to be one of the go-backs," Amanda said.

"Nobody does," Pa said, and the family stood quiet in the mountain wind.

"Begging your pardon," Mr. Cuthbert said. His wife stood behind him. Her face was wet with tears.

"We're going back," he said. "We're going to drop everything and hightail it home. You need livestock," he went on. "We'll only need one ox, and we've got four. Can we make a deal?"

Three new oxen? Now? "We can go on!" Ben couldn't stay quiet any longer. "On to Oregon!"

The rest of the afternoon flew by. Ben helped Pa move both harness and yoke from the Cuthberts' wagon to their own. They hitched all four oxen up and stepped back.

"That's slick!" Ben said. Pa smiled and nodded.

Amanda traded three hours of sewing for two of Mrs. Cuthbert's needles. One woman bought her china, another traded soap for the go-backs' big kettle. The Cuthberts sold the seeds they'd brought to start their Oregon farm.

"Anybody want these books?" Mr. Cuthbert asked.

"I do, sir," Ben said quickly. He wanted to see how other people worked out their words. He picked up *Twice-Told Tales* by Nathaniel Hawthorne and *The Last of the Mohicans* by James Fenimore Cooper. They fit in his trunk beside the journal.

The go-backs gave away their extra rope, guns, and medicines. "We won't be needing them, and you might," Mr. Cuthbert said. When they'd turned their wagon around, nothing was left by the trail but their iron stove.

"Wait!" Zack's grandmother hurried to hand Mr. Cuthbert a card. "Would you mail this to my sister?"

"I should write to Uncle Jeb," Mama said.

"Amy would like to know the baby came healthy."

"Is there anybody here can write? I can't and I want to tell my Betsy I'll marry her for sure."

"Ben can write letters for you," Pete said. "Now let's get this done so we can get to the divide by nightfall."

"Hi-yup!" Pa finally cracked his whip. Four oxen tried to fall into step. The wagon jerked on up the trail.

"Want a ride?" Pete pulled his horse up beside Ben. Together they trotted past the wagons and on toward the sunset. "Here she is." Pete pulled his horse to a stop. "The divide."

Ben looked. The grassy trail stretched ahead and behind. The mountains were all around. "It doesn't look special."

"It is. Every drop of rain that falls behind us runs east to the Atlantic. The rain that falls from here on runs west, all the way to the Pacific Ocean."

The Pacific. The words rang in Ben's ears. Before this summer, he'd never known anyone who'd seen that strange ocean—or these wild mountains, or the deserts. The trail was a world of new places to see, he thought—and to tell others about.

Desert Fire

Water, thought Ben. His foot dragged across the baked soil. If I could only have some water.

Water was all he could think of. He remembered the last rain he'd felt on his face in the South Pass, more than a month ago. He thought about the wild rapids—and the drownings—at the Snake River crossing weeks ago. The sweet spring where they'd filled their barrels days and days ago.

He tried to remember the water fight with the Sioux

Indian boy. That seemed like someone else's life now, not his own. Now there was just heat and sun and sun and thirst.

He lost count of the graves he'd walked past. If I get out of this desert alive, he told himself, I'll never play with water again.

He watched his feet taking step after step across the desert. "Mama, I'm thirsty," Becky cried. It sounded more like a whisper.

"Mama promised us all a swallow of water at the noon break," Ben reminded her. He pictured how it would feel. He wouldn't swallow it all at once. No, he'd hold it in his mouth first. It would feel slick and warm and good against his dry tongue. Then he'd swallow little bits at a time, and rinse all the dust out of his throat.

He licked his lips before he could stop himself. He hated the feel of his dry tongue against the deep cracks in his lips. He didn't want them to start bleeding again.

Becky stumbled and reached out for his hand. He looked down at her. There were streaks through the dust on her cheeks where she'd been crying. A waste of water, he thought.

Beside them, the oxen plodded along. Mama and Pa and Amanda marched in silence beyond the team. The oxen's heads hung low and their eyes looked sunken. Ben reached out and patted Sam's side. Dust sifted through his fingers. Sam's hooves were so dry they had cracked where they pounded the dirt.

"Look, another note," Becky said. Ben shaded his eyes to see where she pointed. A cow skull shimmered in the sun.

"Becky, it's just one more dead pack animal."

Ben plodded on. After all the graves, he thought, it would be nice to read another note from somebody who had come this way and lived. They had found love notes left all along the trail from someone named Kevin to a lady named Kristen. "Help yourself," said notes on top of piles of heavy goods left behind by travelers. Notes that said "Poison water" had saved them from sickness twice.

Best of all, Ben thought, were the books he'd found. "The prairie library," Pete called it. He told Ben, "Leave one behind for each one you take." Ben had read one by Washington Irving while he walked along beside the oxen, and left it for someone else by the Snake River.

He had retold the stories over and over since then. "Do you want to hear about Rip Van Winkle?" he asked Becky. "Or the legend of Sleepy Hollow?" They should think about something besides thirst.

"No," his sister said. "I want to go read the skull."

"So go."

"You have to come, too, Ben. You know what Mama said after the rattler bit Zack's dog . . ."

"Nobody wanders alone," they chanted together as they headed off the trail.

"You're going to feel like a fool," Ben said, "when you see it's just a plain old—" He stopped.

"*No water for two full days' drive.*" Ben read the skull aloud. Below that, the crooked black letters said simply, "*Good luck.*"

"No, no, no!" Becky yelled and started to cry.

"Benjamin," Mama called from the other side of the wagon, "Are you teasing your sister?"

"Mama, you'd better come see this."

A crowd gathered around the skull. "Pete, is this right?" someone asked.

"As I remember it, water should be just one day's ride from here," the mountain man said. "But I could be wrong."

"I'm out of water now," one lady cried. "I think my baby is dying!" The child lay limp in her arms.

"We'll push as far as the oxen can take us tonight," the wagon train's captain decided.

By afternoon, two more horses and an ox had dropped. They left them where they fell and pushed on toward water. The baby died. "Keep rolling," the mother sobbed. "I'll just carry her awhile. We've got to get to water." No one argued. The train moved on.

No water for two full days drive.
Good Luck

Ben was worried about Becky. She kept stumbling beside him. When he took her hand to help her walk, her skin felt dry as dust.

The air cooled toward evening. The wagons didn't stop. The sun was low in the western sky. Still they pushed on. "Smaller swallows this time," Mama warned them. The dipper scraped the bottom of the water barrel. "Make it last."

Pa was carrying Becky now.

"Water!"

"Thank God!" The cries came from the front of the train.

"A water wagon!"

"Thanks be!"

Ben left the team and ran ahead with the others. Water! The crowd rushed down a slope toward a lone wagon sitting in a dry streambed. And stopped.

"WATER, $10 A DIPPERFUL." Zack's father read the first sign aloud. "PAY IN GOLD COIN OR JEWELRY."

"You can't *sell* water!" someone yelled. The crowd rumbled with anger.

A man stepped out from behind the wagon and pointed a pistol at them. "Step right up," he said. "Get in line. Men or children first, it don't matter to me." And he took a dipperful of water and poured it slowly onto the ground.

Ben looked at the dark stain in the sand and licked his cracked lips. They might have enough money for a couple of dippers, since Pa had found work fixing wagons along the way. But Zack's family had no cash at all. What would they do? This wasn't fair!

The crowd began to mutter again. The man shot the gun off over their heads and grabbed another from his belt. The sound of gunfire echoed in the silent, dry hills.

"Stand clear, you snake!"

"Mama!" Ben gasped. His mother held Pa's rifle. It was cocked and pointed at the man's gut.

"Put down the gun, ma'am."

Mama didn't move.

"You're a dead woman, then." Ben saw Pete sneaking around the back of the water wagon. He remembered how many times Pete had snuck up on him. Mama kept talking.

"Go ahead," she said. "Shoot me. But I'll take you down before I die." Ben held his breath.

"Gosh, ma'am," the man said. He lowered his gun an inch—and Pete was on him.

"Mama, you faced him down!" Amanda cried.

"Shoot him!" somebody yelled.

"Nah, hang him!" somebody else said. "Shooting's too good for the likes of him."

Mama strode to the front. Ben had hated it when she had cut her skirts in half and sewed them up almost like pants. It looked right, now.

"We'll deal with him," she turned to the crowd, "after we get our water. Line up here. Children first."

"I just wanted to help my family," the man pleaded. "They're waiting at the springs a half day's drive from here. Our train found a water wagon here, too, sent back by the folks on ahead."

"Did they charge for the water?" Pete asked him.

"Naw. That was my idea. So was the lie I wrote on the skull. My train doesn't know about any of this. Oh, don't tell my kids!" One of the men spit on him.

Ben drank and drank and drank again. "Keep drinking," Pete said. "And get little Becky to drink more, too. When you get this dry, your body forgets how much you need."

The wagon train circled around the water wagon for the night. Pete tied the man onto a horse. "We'll give this snake back to his own family for justice," said Mama. She swung onto the farm horse and set off across the desert at a trot beside Pete.

Ben and his sisters stood with Pa and watched them ride away. The women had been riding like that for a while now, one leg on each side of the horse.

"Is Mama ever going to ride sidesaddle like a real lady again?" Amanda wondered out loud.

Nobody bothered to answer.

Rapids

"The best farmland in the country lies ahead," Pete said, "on the other side of Mount Hood." Ben looked at the huge peak.

"We have to get the wagons over *that?*" one man asked. It was only September 24, and already the mountaintops all around were white with snow. Mount Hood alone seemed to fill half the sky.

"Nope. The trail ends down at a town on the Columbia River. You've got to make a choice there.

You can raft your gear down the river or carry it for three weeks into the valley."

Pete's voice went on, but Ben's mind stopped. *The end?* The end of the Oregon Trail? The end of the walking? The thirst? It had seemed like the trail would go on forever.

"Both ways are dangerous," Pete was saying, "rafting your goods down the river or carrying them down the trail. It's your choice. Winter's coming, so you'd better make up your minds."

Quick thinking is always easy for Pa, Ben thought. He walked with the others back to the wagons. Pa's choice to come west had been sudden. It was right after the asthma had hit. And Pa had bought their wagon the first time he saw it.

"So what are we going to do, raft to our farm or keep rolling?" Ben asked. He helped his father put the oxen in harness.

"Don't know," Pa said. Ben's arms dropped to his sides. Pa pushed his knee into Sam's side. "Get over, you stupid thing," he said. The big ox finally moved, and the yoke fell into place. Pa glared at the team and shook his head. "I knew for sure when we left home that I wanted to be a farmer. But now . . ."

If Pa didn't know, nobody did! "You can't be thinking of going back!" Ben said, and held his breath. All those miles. All those months.

"Wish we could," Pa mumbled. Ben stood, stunned.

"You came all this way for me and you're sorry?" He couldn't bear it.

"For *you?* Whatever gave you that idea?" Pa said. "*I* wanted a farm. Or I thought I did." He picked up the whip. Sam snorted and shook his head. Pa whipped the oxen and the team began pulling for the day. His face looked tired and sad. Ben let the team walk past. He let Mama and Amanda and Becky walk past.

"One last ride to the front, Bear Cub?" Pete pulled up beside Ben.

They rode silently along the trail. "My kind of country," Pete said once. Ben nodded. They looked around at peak after peak, stretching as far as they could see.

Riding around a bend, Ben looked down at a broad river and caught his breath. "The Columbia?"

Pete nodded. "That town down there is called The Dalles," he said.

The end, Ben thought. The roar of rapids rose to meet them as they rode down the mountainside into town.

"Why, Pete, you old fur thief!" a man called out as they trotted down the main street. He was dressed like Pete, all leather and fur and fringe. "You been out showing folks the elephant again?" The mountain man bit off a huge wad of tobacco and chewed.

"Almost everybody got to see their elephant this time through, and it changed them plenty." Pete got off his horse. "Fourteen died trying, though."

"How'd it happen this time? Them durn Indians?"

Pete's grin showed through his beard. "Of course not." The grin died. "Like always, we lost the ones that got clumsy with guns or animals, or around water. Then there was the cholera. . . ."

Ben pictured the graves along the way.

Pete's friend spit into the river. "I suppose you'll be heading back for another train?"

"Naw," Pete said. "The trail is getting too crowded for the likes of us, Jeb. I get to missing my mountains. And my tribe."

"You going back to them?"

"Most likely. Buy you a drink?"

Jeb spit again. "You have to ask?" The men wandered over into a saloon. Ben walked up to the swinging door and stopped. The sour smell of beer and perfume and burned stew made him wish for mountain air again.

He stood in the mud of The Dalles' main street. The buildings were all log cabins. Dozens of wagons lined the road. Chickens and pigs and people were everywhere.

Three boys about Ben's age came out of the cabin that said DRY GOODS. "Howdy, newcomer," one said to

Ben. A pair of women walked past. Both of them were wearing split skirts like Mama's. A girl about the size of Becky chased a hoop down the middle of the dirt road.

Ben walked faster. Now he looked at every building in town. With all these people, Ben thought, there should be houses fresh with the smell of new wood. Houses like Pa could build. And stores. In his mind, Ben could already see them. A chemist for medicines. A blacksmith. A candlemaker. Ben turned around when he reached the last log cabin at the edge of town. He hurried toward the saloon again. He couldn't wait to get back to the wagons. To tell his father what he'd seen.

There were no carpenters in The Dalles.

Not yet, anyhow.

"Pete," Ben finally had to ask on the long way back up the trail, "did I see the elephant?"

"You don't know?" was Pete's answer. "You faced down one of the biggest elephants in these parts."

Ben looked up at Mount Hood and wondered what Pete could be talking about. He knew he hadn't been attacked or starved. He hadn't caught the cholera like Amanda. He hadn't gotten a snakebite or fallen into a river. How could he be proud of something if he didn't have a name for it? Maybe Pete was talking about the desert and the awful thirst. It was going to be nice,

Ben thought, to live where you could always hear rushing water.

"Pa!" Ben yelled when they got back to the wagon train. "Mama!" He jumped off Pete's horse and ran to join his family.

September 24, 1845, Ben wrote that evening. *The last night on the trail. We finally made it to Oregon!* That was in big letters. *But we won't have a farm here, after all. Pa sold or traded away the cows and the team, the seed, and the plow this afternoon. Zack's father traded his tools for most of it.*

Ben looked off into the darkness toward the sound of the rapids and smiled. Mama and Pa had gone down to The Dalles. Pa had been whistling. By now, they were buying the wood to build a house. Pa's would be as new as the town—as new as Oregon. He had made up his mind quickly, after all.

Amanda is sewing by the fire, Ben wrote. *Becky is already asleep. I am writing.* That looked a little silly, but Ben left it. He looked back over the months of journal pages.

He laughed when he read the parts about how hard he had thought life was back on the prairie last spring. They sounded like a stranger's words. But he'd never seen a mountain or a desert. How little he knew then! He had hated writing back then, and it showed.

It had gotten easier when he started drawing

pictures. He found the one of the buffalo and the one of the Sioux boy. He stopped at the sketch of the graves of the three Cuthbert children.

Ben read the quotes he had copied from books he had picked up and left behind again. He poked his finger on a cactus spine he had stuck into a page to save. He squeezed out a drop of blood and let it drip beside his picture of a cactus. "I wonder if I'll ever see a desert again," he said out loud.

"Why ever would you want to?" Amanda didn't even look up from her sewing.

In the space left on the page, Ben sketched a last picture of Pete, all fringes and beard and grin. It felt good to have a place to put down his thoughts now. To draw. To remember. He would never tell Zack that, of course, or Amanda.

Finally he wrote *The End* in fancy letters and snapped the journal shut.

Ben sat looking into the fire. Zack was going on. Ben wasn't. He didn't want the adventures to be over.

Ben thought about the boys he had seen in The Dalles. One had even said "howdy." Maybe there were more adventures ahead after all. And there were plenty of empty pages left in the book.

Ben opened the journal again and turned back to Pete's picture. He crossed out *The End* neatly and closed the book with a smile.

Ben helped the men get Zack's family's huge raft off the riverbank. "Push!" someone said. "Push! What in tarnation you got on this boat?"

"Two farms," Ben said, and grinned. "The one we didn't want and the one Zack did."

Finally the raft slipped into the water. It dipped and leveled. Then it was off, pulled by the fast current. Ben raised his arm to wave and stood panting.

He felt his chest get tight, but that didn't scare him anymore. He made himself relax, almost without thinking. Almost. And then Ben smiled.

He knew the name of his elephant.

ABOUT THIS BOOK

People really did talk about "seeing the elephant" on the Oregon Trail. The six hard months it took to travel the trail's 2,000 miles tested everyone who made the journey. The trail opened the west—and a new way of living—for the United States.

Meriwether Lewis and William Clark were the first to map parts of the Oregon Trail, in 1805. Other explorers followed. Trappers and mountain men carried their furs along the trail to trading posts. A single wagon pushed through in the 1830s. In 1841, the first wagon train carried 24 people to the Oregon Territory. Almost 1,000 made it through in 1843. By 1860, *a quarter of a million* settlers had followed the trail to Oregon or taken the south branch to California.

Why did they go? They went for adventure, for a fresh start, for their health, to escape the nation's arguments about slavery or their own problems with money or the law, for free farmland—everyone had a different reason. People who had made the trip wrote back east about the beautiful scenery, the sweet, rich farmlands, and (after 1849) gold. The writers sometimes warned of attacks by Native Americans, whom they called Indians. Actually, those natives were more helpful than dangerous to pioneers, at least in the early years of the trail. Travelers reported snakes and storms and swollen rivers, too. These all made for good stories, but they weren't the biggest killers on the trail.

Falls from animals and wagons, accidental gunshots, and illness took far more lives. Many trips were not very exciting at all—just long. Six months spent walking over prairies, mountains, and deserts is a long, long time. Travelers on the trail helped each other, leaving notes and sending water wagons back after dry crossings. Women had to become strong and independent to survive the journey. They seldom went back to being dainty little ladies.

Ben and his family are made up. So are Pete and Zack and the rest. But thousands of real people had the same troubles and joys along the trail.

To write this book, I read about the trail and I studied maps and photographs of the country. I worked from old sources, too. In a library at Yale University in New Haven, Connecticut, I read diaries kept on the trail. Holding these journals in my hands, looking at the sketches, and reading the words was like talking to the pioneers themselves.

These were brave people. Some were newlyweds. Some were traveling alone. Some had small children or were old. A few, like Ben, were facing illness. All shared the dream of starting anew in the West—and all were willing to risk their lives for that dream.

K. V. K.